BOGUS BEAUCHARD
And The Bloody Benders

a Screenplay

Karin Humbolt

The Reynolds Publishing Company

Overland Park, Kansas

BOGUS BEAUCHARD And The Bloody Benders

Written by Karin Humbolt

Copyright © 2019 by Karin Humbolt

Library of Congress Control Number: 2019909928

ISBN: 978-0-9665128-6-1

Published and distributed in the United States of America by:

The Reynolds Publishing Company
P.O. Box 13535
Overland Park, Kansas 66282

Printed in the United States of America

FOREWARD

BOGUS BEAUCHARD And The Bloody Benders

Post-Civil War Kansas, like much of the country, ached from war wounds … physical, emotional, monetary, and with family members torn asunder. Women were left widows … children were orphaned and homeless. As a teenager, I visited Dodge City, Kansas' Boot Hill. Instead of the small town "tourist trap" that I imagined, I saw that the Boot Hill museum was a wonderful source of research and material for the western writer. There is where I first learned the story of post-war victims. Many children and women found it necessary to turn to prostitution. And while most eventually married, townsmen and farmers, this was their lot in life. And so is the struggle of this story's sixteen-year old Tanya McClelland.

While murder and mayhem are part of *Bogus Beauchard And The Bloody Benders*, the real story is the struggle of post-Civil War orphans and widows. Tanya

McClelland is such an orphan. Scarred by the death of her beloved father what was she to do? Her answer is Bogus Beauchard.

While Bogus Beauchard and Tanya McClelland are fictional characters, the Bender clan existed in real life. With my enthusiasm and penchant for history and research, I set out to learn what happened to the notorious Bender clan who served, tormented, and murdered during their life in 1870's Southeast Kansas. For every death bed confession told to a son or grandson, there are like numbered stories of the fate of the Benders.

Know that *Bogus Beauchard And The Bloody Benders* is a screenplay-novel. For those not acquainted with screenplay format, imagine, while you are reading, that you are watching a film. Note that EXT. means exterior and INT. means interior. V.O. means voice over. And CUT TO and FADE OUT mean that the scene has ended.

Read, enjoy, and discover Tanya, Bogus Beauchard and the Bloody Benders.

K.H.

FADE IN:

EXT. KANSAS CITY - DECEMBER 1936 - LATE AFTERNOON

The wealthy residential sector of the city is covered with snow and decorated for Christmas. A NEWSPAPER BOY throws a paper hard against the beveled glass front door of a mansion.

ANGLE ON

The front door opens and GEORGE THE BUTLER appears. He scowls at the Boy as he collects the newspaper.

INT. HOUSE – DAY

The Butler strides through the magnificent house, past an elaborate Christmas tree, to closed mahogany doors. He knocks, then enters.

INT. LIBRARY - DAY

A well-dressed, ELDERLY WOMAN, sits by a fireplace, her face turned from view. The Butler sets the paper on a table next to the woman.

> ELDERLY WOMAN
> George, have you seen my spectacles?

The Butler retrieves gold rimmed glasses from above the fireplace and hands them to the Elderly Woman.

                    BUTLER
        Your great-grandson rang that he wishes
        to see you this evening. Before the family
        "sets in for the holidays" as he called it.

                    ELDERLY WOMAN
                      (laughs)
        There's more of me in that boy than both
        my sons. All they'll want to talk about is
        their latest business venture!
                (reaching for the newspaper)
        Stir the fire, George.

The Elderly Woman scans the headlines as the Butler tends
the fire.

PAN IN

Newspaper headline. "Sixty Year Gold Search Continues"

                    ELDERLY WOMAN
                   (intake of breath)
        See that cook prepares the boy's favorite
        dishes.

                    BUTLER
                    Yes, Madam.

Butler leaves the room. The Elderly Woman adjusts her
glasses.

                    ELDERLY WOMAN
                      (reading)
        More than sixty years ago, three government

                        2

ELDERLY WOMAN
(cont.)
agents left Fort Leavenworth for ...

DISSOLVE TO:

EXT. SOUTHEAST KANSAS PRAIRIE - 1870'S – DAY

WILSON, JANNER and PACKINS, government agents, cross
the prairie on horseback, followed by two packed mules.
The hot summer sun slows progress to a walk through the
rolling hills. Wilson, the older and leader of the three,
wipes perspiration from his face. The men rein their horses
at a tree-lined river bank.

RIVER BANK

The men tie their horses and the mules to the blackjack
oaks and cottonwood trees that line the river. The SOUND
OF LOCUSTS IS LOUD. Wilson double checks the knot tying
the mules.

WILSON
Good camp site.
(laughs)
If the locusts don't keep us awake half the night.

Janner remains silent. Packins, fidgets with the reins on his
horse, laughs.

WILSON
(over his shoulder)
Janner, you and Packins make camp.

                    WILSON
                  (continued)
        I'll be cooling myself down at the river.

                    PACKINS
                   (wistfully)
            Seems a shame, all that gold.

Wilson gives Packins a stern look. Janner glares at Packins.

                    PACKINS
          Two hundred and fifty thousand would
          go a long ways ... split by three.

                    WILSON
          Shut your mouth! We've got a job to do.
          Set up camp!

Wilson walks to the river. Packins gives Janner a pleading
look which Janner shrugs off before following Wilson.

RIVER

Wilson kneels shirtless by the river's edge, splashing
himself. A darkened shadow fills the water in front of him.
Shading his eyes from the sun, Wilson looks up. A puzzled
expression crosses his face.

SOUND OF GUNSHOT

Blood streaks the river red until the current carries
Wilson's body down stream.

                        4

ANOTHER ANGLE

HOLSTERED GUN. The SOUND OF LOCUSTS GROWS
LOUDER.

DISSOLVE TO:

EXT. BENDER INN - DUSK

Two large hills rise above the prairie casting shadows on to
the Osage Trail that winds past the Bender Inn. The inn is a
small 25 x 16-foot log cabin with a crude wooden sign
above the door. To the front of the cabin is a water trough
and small livestock shed. An orchard is in the back.

OLD MAN BENDER, a crude-looking man in his sixties, well
over six feet tall, sits at a bench holding a bible. Glancing
up, his attention focuses on the nearby Osage Trail.

ANGLE ON

Janner and Packins on horseback, lead Wilson's horse and
the saddle laden pack mules.

ANGLE ON

OLD MAN BENDER
(German accent)

Kate!

KATE BENDER, a tall, dark haired woman in her early
twenties, appears in the cabin doorway. Kate is sultry and
voluptuous. Kate casts a contemptuous look on Old Man

Bender. He indicates the trail. Kate sees Janner and
Packins riding toward the inn.

                    KATE BENDER
                (shouting into the cabin)
            Two more plates for the table, Ma.

JOHN BENDER, an anemic looking, red-haired man in his
twenties, walks from behind the cabin carrying a shovel.
Bender's hands are covered with dirt. He approaches Kate,
who gives him the same contemptuous look she gave Old
Man Bender. John Bender's mouth twitches as he sees the
approaching riders.

                    JOHN BENDER
                    (giggles)
            Business shore has been good, huh, Kate?

                    KATE BENDER
            Shut up!

Janner and Packins dismount their horses. Kate
approaches the men.

                    KATE BENDER
            Evenin'. I'm Kate Bender. This is Pa and
            that's my brother, John.

Old Man Bender grunts then resumes his bible reading.

                    KATE BENDER
            Don't mind him. He don't speak much English.

Packins takes off his hat and ogles Kate.

PACKINS
Pleased to meet you, Ma'am. My name
is ... Jones and, this is Miller.

John Bender giggles. Janner glares at Bender then leads
the horses to the water trough.

JANNER
We need supplies.

KATE BENDER
(airily)
We have all the supplies you need. We
also have fine food and comfortable
lodging for the night.

JANNER
Supplies and supper's all we need.

Packins eyes Kate.

PACKINS
Ah, let's spend the night. My rump's sore.

Kate pushes John Bender toward the horses.

KATE BENDER
Quit your gawking. Tend to these
gentlemen's horses.

Bender moves toward the horses.

                    JOHN BENDER
          Shore got them mules packed.

Janner steps in front of Bender.

                      JANNER
                     (tersely)
          I'll tend to 'em!
                   (to Packins)
          Get the supplies.
                    (to Kate)
          You bring the grub outside.

Kate bristles.

                     PACKINS
          No need to insult the lady. Let's eat inside.

                      JANNER
          I'm stayin' out here.

                   KATE BENDER
          Suit yourself.

Kate leads the way into the cabin. Packins and John
Bender follow. Old Man Bender gives Janner an empty
stare, then he walks into the cabin.

                                              CUT TO:

INT. BENDER INN – NIGHT

OLD WOMAN BENDER, a female version of her husband,

cooks over a wood-fired stove. Shelves of groceries line the walls of the small dirty cabin. Packins sits at a table, his back to the canvass. He admires Kate when she brings a plate of food.

                    KATE BENDER
          There's plenty more.

                    PACKINS
          Thank you, Ma'am.

Kate tolerates his hand on her arm for a moment. John Bender sits down across the table from Packins, grinning. Old Man Bender steps behind the canvass.

                    KATE BENDER
          I'll take some food out to your
          partner. Then, I'll be back to wait
          on you.

                    PACKINS
          Yes, Ma'am. You do that.

Kate takes an apron off a hook and puts it on. She piles a plate high with food. She nods to Old Woman Bender, who turns and stares cow-like at Packins.

EXT. BENDER INN – NIGHT

Kate walks through the lighted doorway to where Janner finishes feeding the horses. Janner takes the plate of food Kate hands him, ignoring her provocative gaze. Kate stretches, then leans against a pack mule, watching Janner eat.

> KATE BENDER
> Thank heaven for the nights.

Janner looks at Kate, then pointedly at her cleavage. He continues eating.

> KATE BENDER
> The cool air is what I mean. Or
> what little of it there is.
> (beat)
> Course, sometimes the nights
> get real hot.

Janner looks at her. Kate smiles. She turns and runs a hand over the saddle bags.

> KATE BENDER
> Traveling far?

> JANNER
> Far enough.

Janner sets down his plate and brushing past Kate, tightens the cinch on a pack mule.

> JANNER
> Time to be heading out.

Kate puts an arm around Janner's neck.

                    KATE BENDER
                      (husky)
          What's the rush?

Kate smiles and runs her fingers through Janner's hair.

                    KATE BENDER
                    (continued)
          The bed's soft.

Janner puts an arm around Kate's waist.

                      JANNER
          I bet the nights do get hot.

As Janner pulls Kate close, a SHRILL SCREAM IS HEARD from
the cabin. Janner looks up as Packins staggers to the
doorway, hands at the back of his head. Packins SCREAMS
again as Old Man Bender strikes him with a hatchet.

Janner reaches for his gun as Kate stabs him with a butcher
knife. He back hands Kate, levels the gun toward the cabin
and fires.

Janner grabs the reins of the pack mules, mounts his own
horse and whips the animals into a run.

Kate staggers to her feet, attempts to run after Janner,
then stops and looks back at John and Old Man Bender.
Her face contorts with anger.

                    KATE BENDER
          Must I do everything! Go after him!

The Bender Men obey, running toward the shed. Kate stares at the darkened Osage Trail, the SOUND OF HORSE HOOVES NOW BARELY AUDIBLE.

CUT TO:

EXT. VERDIGRIS RIVER – SUNRISE

The sky is gray with thick rain clouds and the SOUND OF LOCUSTS IS NEARLY DEAFENING. VICTOR MC CLELLAND, a tall man in his fifties, makes his way down the steep river bank.

Except for the tattered Confederate officer's jacket, McClelland is dressed like any poor farmer of the time. McClelland carries a homemade fishing pole and shovel. His progress is hampered by the blackjack oak trees that line the river bottom, and the tuberculosis cough that every few strides rankles his body.

McClelland abruptly dodges behind several blackjacks and a tangle of bramble. He peers through the brush and sees Janner, his shirt caked with blood, digging with a tin plate. Suppressing a cough, McClelland crouches to the ground.

Janner struggles, his breathing labored, as he furiously digs the soil. LIGHT RAIN BEGINS TO FALL. McClelland claps a hand to his mouth as he struggles to keep from coughing.

Janner digs faster. THUNDER SOUNDS. McClelland coughs violently as the THUNDER CONTINUES. Janner climbs out of the hole and opens a saddle bag. McClelland watches transfixed as Janner strokes a gold bar. Janner replaces the

12

gold and shoves the saddle bags into the hole. McClelland closes his eyes and holds his breath to fight off another coughing spasm.

Janner packs and smooths the soil. He pulls a knife from a sheath and carves the bark of a blackjack tree.

McClelland lies in the brush coughing uncontrollably as the THUNDER INTENSIFIES. As his coughing subsides, McClelland rises. Seeing that Janner is gone, McClelland climbs the riverbank.

McClelland reaches the clearing in time to see Janner disappear on horseback to the south. As the rain begins to pour, McClelland heads back toward the river, whistling "DIXIE" until a coughing spasm seizes him.

                                                    CUT TO:

EXT. KANSAS STATE PENITENTIARY AT LEAVENWORTH - A YEAR LATER- DAY

INT. WARDEN'S OFFICE- DAY

A GUARD shoves WILLIAM BEAUCHARD into the room. Beauchard's appearance attests to his years of incarceration. He is thin, dirty and his long hair and beard, unkept. Beauchard's sharp eyes miss nothing and although well acquainted with prison life, his manner is insolent. CUTLER, a hired ruffian, is seated behind the warden's desk. Cutler's smile fails to hide his callous nature. Cutler's THREE HENCHMEN stand.

CUTLER
Howdy, Beauchard.

BEAUCHARD
(a slight Southern accent)
Where's the Warden?

CUTLER
He stepped out for a bit... My name's Cutler.

BEAUCHARD
Well now, seeing how we've
been formerly introduced ... what
do you want with me?

CUTLER
(chuckles)
Formerly introduced.
(all business)
Beauchard, tell me about your
old cell mate.

BEAUCHARD
Janner?
(shrugs)
Wasn't much turn out for his funeral.

FIRST HENCHMAN shoves Beauchard against the wall.

BEAUCHARD
What's it to you?

                    CUTLER
          Janner had something that belonged
          to my boss. My boss thinks you might
          know where it is.
                    (beat)
          So, do I.

                    BEAUCHARD
          I don't rightly know what you're
          getting at mister.

                    CUTLER
          You and Janner were cellmates for
          quite a spell. Don't tell me he never
          mentioned the gold?

                    BEAUCHARD
          What gold?

SECOND HENCHMAN punches Beauchard in the stomach.
Beauchard falls to his knees gasping for air. THIRD
HENCHMAN aims a foot at Beauchard.

                    BEAUCHARD
                    (shouts)
          Wait!
                    (gasps)
          Janner did mention something
          about gold. Hell, that's all he
          talked about.

                    15

                    CUTLER
        Well, then. Maybe he told you
        where he hid it?

                  BEAUCHARD
        Maybe.

Cutler nods to Henchman, who kicks Beauchard.

                  BEAUCHARD
        It won't do any good to me kill me.

                    CUTLER
        Maybe I'd get a charge watching
        you die.

Beauchard slowly stands.

                  BEAUCHARD
        Something tells me your boss prefers me alive.

Cutler straightens in the chair.

                    CUTLER
        Now that all depends on what
        you have to offer.

                  BEAUCHARD
        I've got a map.
                (taps forehead)
        Up here. And the only way you're
        gettin' it, is by setting me free.

                    CUTLER
          Tell me where the gold is and I'll
          let you out.

                    BEAUCHARD
          In a wooden box.

                    CUTLER
          Not before my men slice you like
          a steer.

Beauchard smiles, shaking his head.

                    BEAUCHARD
          You can't do anything to me that
          hasn't already been done. As far
          as dying, well that'd be a comfort.
                    (beat)
          You want your gold, get me out of
          here. I'll need a good horse, supplies
          and cash. Oh, yeah, ... two revolvers
          ... reliable ... a rifle and a shotgun.

Cutler's face hardens as he stares at Beauchard.

                                        CUT TO:

EXT. TOWN MAIN STREET – DAY

TANYA MC CLELLAND, a girl of sixteen, slight of build and
pretty in an awkward adolescent way, sits on horseback in
front of the Hotel Cafe, reading a dime novel. She is
oblivious to the congested street filled with teams of
horses and oxen pulling wagons, HORSEBACK RIDERS and

PEDESTRIANS scurrying across the mud road to the shops, cafes, and saloons that line the road. Tanya's clothing, a worn calico dress over trousers, although thrice mended, is clean and neat. Hanging by a ribbon around her neck is a faded blue bonnet. Tanya is a contradiction between her Southern upbringing and the reality of homestead life in southeast Kansas. She speaks with a pronounced Southern accent.

                    TANYA
                 (to herself)
        Jean Louie passionately embraced Violet.
                   (sighs)
Tanya turns the page.

                    TANYA
          His lips traveled ...

            JAMES WARREN (V.O.)
               (clears throat)
          Must be a good book.

Tanya looks up embarrassed, quickly closes the book and slides it into a saddle bag. JAMES WARREN, a young lawyer smiles at her, as does Warren's employer, COLONEL ALEXANDER YORK, and the Colonel's brother, DR. JONATHAN YORK. The York brothers are in their mid-thirties.

                    TANYA
          Good afternoon, Colonel York, Dr. York,
          ... James Warren.

COLONEL YORK
Good afternoon, Miss McClelland. In
town for some shopping?

TANYA
No, sir. I heard there was a cattle buyer
in town from Abilene. Thought he might take
the noon meal here at the cafe.

DR. YORK
More likely than not, he's across the street.

Tanya looks across the street at the Michaels' Lady
Saloon.

TANYA
In the saloon?

COLONEL YORK
I'm sure my brother's only joking.

Dr. York shakes his head skeptically.

COLONEL YORK
(cont.)
Why don't you leave word for him
at the hotel? His name is Jessie Wells.

TANYA
Thank you, Colonel York.

James Warren helps Tanya as she gets off her horse.

TANYA

By the way Colonel York, I'd like to tell
you what a comfort it is to have you as this
county's representative in the senate. I
know you'll be looking out for the best
interest of all citizens.

COLONEL YORK

Thank you for your words of confidence.
I only hope I can help put a stop to the
abominable corruption that's plaguing
Kansas.

TANYA

I'm sure you will.

COLONEL YORK

Thank you. It's time I returned to
the office. Coming James Warren?

JAMES WARREN

In a moment, sir.

COLONEL YORK
(to Tanya)

While you're in town, call on Mrs.
York, she's always delighted to see
you, Miss McClelland.

TANYA

Thank you.

DR. YORK
Good day.

After the York brothers walk away, James Warren, tongue
tied, looks at Tanya and sighs. He then smiles awkwardly.

JAMES WARREN
Tanya, what's this about a cattle buyer?

TANYA
I'm going to sell my herd.

JAMES WARREN
A few dozen cattle is hardly a herd.

TANYA
It's a herd to me.   And I intend to sell it!

JAMES WARREN
Why don't you let me handle the
transaction?

Tanya rolls her eyes.

JAMES WARREN
I am a lawyer.

TANYA
And a very fine lawyer, James Warren.

JAMES WARREN
I worry about you, Tanya. You're

                    JAMES WARREN
                      (cont.)
              vulnerable without your pa. I don't
              want anyone to take advantage of you.

                       TANYA
              What a sweet thing to say, James.

Tanya looks across the street, more concerned with who's
going in and out of the saloon than the boy talking to her.

                    JAMES WARREN
              Tanya, have you considered my suggestion?

                       TANYA
         Why?

                    JAMES WARREN
                (taking Tanya's hand in his)
              You know the answer to that as
              well as anyone. You can't run a ranch
              by yourself.

Tanya yanks her hand from his grasp.

                       TANYA
              You have no right to talk to me
              like that! The only reason I know
              as you call it, is because everyone in
              the territory says the same thing. I'm
              sick of their talk.

                    JAMES WARREN
                     (frustrated)
        Tanya!

                       TANYA
                      (loud)
        What am I supposed to do in town?
        The only two jobs around here for a
        woman are clerking... or working in
        the saloon. I'd so hate being a clerk
        and I'm not exactly qualified for the other.

James Warren winces, and his face turns red as MRS.
WATTS, a well-dressed matron and her daughters CINDY
and LUCY approach.

                    JAMES WARREN
        Good afternoon, Mrs. Watts. Miss
        Cindy. Miss Lucy.

                 MRS. AND MISSES WATTS
        Good afternoon, James Warren.
                      (beat)
        Tanya.

Tanya pretends not to notice their stares of disapproval of
her clothing, but, purses her lips when walking past the
WATTS GIRLS laugh.

                       TANYA
        Prissy snots! I've got a good mind to .....
                 (noting James' expression)
        You're no better! You and your insults!

                         23

JAMES WARREN
Tanya, never on this earth would
I intentionally insult you. I merely
meant there must be a solution to your
predicament.
(taking her hand once more)
It's not safe for you out there by yourself.

TANYA
(patting his cheek)
You worry too much, James.

JAMES WARREN
I must get to the office. Why don't
you meet me at the house at four
o'clock. We'll have tea with Mother.

TANYA
(noting her mended clothing)
I'm hardly dressed for calling.

JAMES WARREN
Uhhh. You look fine.

TANYA
Your mother doesn't like me.

JAMES WARREN
Nonsense.

TANYA
No, it's not. She always gets a
pinched look whenever she sees me.

                    JAMES WARREN
          You exaggerate.
               (runs hand through his hair)
          It's ... just that ... if you weren't so all fired
          Southern.

                         TANYA
          I knew it!

                    JAMES WARREN
          The war was bad for anyone living along
          the border. People want to move on.

                         TANYA
          I can't help what I am. My father was an
          officer in the Confederate army. My mother
          came from a very old family. Before the war,
          we lived in a house that made yours look like a
          shanty.

                    JAMES WARREN
          You're living in the past.

James tries to embrace Tanya, but Tanya pushes away.

                         TANYA
          Leave me alone, James.

Tanya dashes across the mud road to the Michael's Lady
Saloon.

                                        CUT TO:

EXT. SALOON ALLEY – DAY

Attempting to avoid being seen, Tanya enters the alley glancing from side to side. A young PROSTITUTE, a girl Tanya's age or younger, exits a tiny dilapidated room. Momentarily, the two girls face each other. One face painted and pathetic, the other terrified at the prospect of similar circumstances.

A BABY CRIES from inside the Prostitute's room. An expression of motherly concern crosses the Prostitute's face before it's replaced with that of a frightened adolescent. The Prostitute rushes past. Tanya shivers, takes a deep breath and walks into the saloon.

CUT TO:

INT. MICHAEL'S LADY SALOON - DAY

Tanya enters the poorly lit saloon.

> SALOON KEEPER
> What you want, girl?

> TANYA
> I... I .... I'm ....

> SALOON KEEPER
> Speak up! Ain't you ever been in
> a saloon before?

> CUSTOMERS
> (laughter)

TANYA
I heard a cattle buyer by the name of Jessie
Wells was here.

JESSIE WELLS (V.O.)
I'm Wells.

JESSIE WELLS, a tough cattle driver, sits at a poker table
playing cards with CUSTOMERS. Seated alone at a nearby
table is Beauchard, civilian clothed, wearing a gun, but still
with long hair and beard. Beauchard, although sketching a
drawing, observes everything. Seated in a far corner is
John Bender.

TANYA
Mr. Wells, my name is Tanya McClelland.
I understand you're in town to buy cattle.

JESSIE WELLS
I am.

TANYA
I have a ranch along the Osage Trail,
near the bend in the Verdigris River.

Beauchard straightens in his chair.

TANYA
(cont.)
I have some cattle I'd like to sell you.

JESSIE WELLS
How come your pa isn't here?

                    TANYA
          My father died last summer.

                  JESSIE WELLS
          Sorry, kid.... How many head you got?

                    TANYA
          Forty-two give or take.

                  JESSIE WELLS
          Longhorns?

                    TANYA
          Yes, sir.

                   CUSTOMER
                   (snicker)
          Rebel longhorns.

Tanya scowls at the Customer.

                  JESSIE WELLS
          I'll pay you five dollars a head.

                    TANYA
                   (dismayed)
          Five dollars?

                  JESSIE WELLS
          It's a rough trail to Dodge City. Full
          of rustlers, Indians and wolves.

ANGLE ON

Beauchard puts away his sketch pad.

                    BEAUCHARD
          Is that why you're getting thirty-two
          dollars a head in Dodge?

                    JESSIE WELLS
               (glaring at Beauchard)
          What makes you an expert?

                    BEAUCHARD
          Common knowledge. Chicago
          buyers are paying thirty-two to
          thirty-five per head.

                    JESSIE WELLS
          It's a long trail between here and
          Dodge. A man's entitled to a profit
          for his labors.

                    BEAUCHARD
          So's a young girl.

                    JESSIE WELLS
          Mind your own business. The little
          lady and I were doing okay until you
          butted in.

                    TANYA
          I don't mind.

                    JESSIE WELLS
          Anyhow, I'm not buying many cattle.

                    BEAUCHARD
        Five minutes ago, you said you'd buy
        all the cattle you could get your hands on.

                    JESSIE WELLS
        For the right price. What's it to you
        anyhow?

                    BEAUCHARD
        Just want to see the girl get a fair deal.

Beauchard removes a tobacco pouch and rolls a cigarette.

                    BEAUCHARD
                    (pause)
        You being short of cattle and all.

                    JESSIE WELLS
                    (to Tanya)
        Ten dollars a head.

                    TANYA
        Twenty.

                    JESSIE WELLS
        Twelve.

                    TANYA
        Gotta have eighteen.

                    JESSIE WELLS
        I'll give you fifteen a head, and that's
        my last offer.

TANYA
Sold.

EXT. MAIN STREET – DAY

John Bender runs after Tanya as she walks to her horse.

JOHN BENDER
Hey, hey, Tanya. Looks like you're
gonna have some money.

TANYA
(continuing walking)
That's right, John.

Tanya pulls a sheet of paper from her saddle bag and pins it
to a hand bill post. Bender looks over her shoulder.

JOHN BENDER
What ya got?

TANYA
A notice for field help.

JOHN BENDER
(giggles)
What for?

TANYA
Watermelons ....

JOHN BENDER
You're sure gonna have lots of money
when them melons come in. Between

31

                    JOHN BENDER
                      (cont'd)
          them and your cattle, why you ......

                 KATE BENDER (V.O.)
          John Bender! Why are you standing
          around gabbing?

Kate Bender stands outside the cafe, wearing a food
stained waitress apron. She glares at Bender.

                    KATE BENDER
          I bet you haven't gotten those
          supplies yet! Hurry up, I'm ready
          to get out of this slop house.

                    JOHN BENDER
          Tanya and I were jawing about when
          she sells her cattle. And she's got an
          advertisement up there now, right
          alongside of yours, Kate.

Kate looks at Tanya's sign.

                    KATE BENDER
          Watermelons, huh?

                    JOHN BENDER
          Tanya's gonna have lots of money
          when the melons get ripe. And she
          just cut a deal with a cattle buyer
          from Dodge.

Kate looks at Tanya amiably.

> KATE BENDER
> Have you seen my advertisement?
> I'm making lots of money these
> days as a faith healer and spiritualist.

Kate sees Tanya's dubious expression.

> KATE BENDER
> This job's only temporary until I
> build my cliental. I'm doing well
> consulting some very wealthy citizens.
> Then there's my long-time client, a
> very important politician. I may even
> marry him.
>   (beat)
> When you get your cattle money you
> ought to come out to our farm for a
> seance.

> TANYA
> I've got to get home.

> KATE BENDER
> If you need help with your
> watermelons, John's available.

Bender grins.

> TANYA
> I don't know.

                    JOHN BENDER
          Hey, I could start real soon. How
          about....

Beauchard steps in front of Bender and rips off Tanya's
poster.

                    BEAUCHARD
          Job's taken.

                    KATE BENDER
          You ought to hire someone you
          know, not a stranger. He looks no
          better than a pea picker.

                    BEAUCHARD
                    (to Kate)
          You better get back to your biscuits.
               (handing a sheet of paper to Tanya)
          For you.

CLOSE SHOT

A pen and ink sketch of Tanya.

ANGLE ON

                    TANYA
          It's a wonderful likeness.
               (looking to the signature)
          I bet you could make a better
          living sketching than tending fields
          ... Mister .....

BEAUCHARD
Beauchard. Don't count on it, Miss
McClelland. Are you ready to head
to your place. I'm ready to get started.

TANYA
All right... it's a deal.

With one look at Kate Bender and then to John Bender,
Beauchard walks to his packed horse. Tanya whistles a few
bars of "DIXIE" as she mounts her horse. As Tanya and
Beauchard ride out of town, Kate watches them, a mixture
of dislike and envy on her face.

CUT TO:

EXT. MC CLELLAND HOMESTEAD – DAY

The two-story sawn-lumber house with its numerous
windows and doors seems out of place on the isolated
prairie. There are small sheds, a barn, water well and a
wood lot near the edge of trees that follow the riverbank.
A short distance from the house is a small family cemetery
with two headstones. Beauchard and Tanya work in the
distant watermelon field.

WATERMELON FIELD

Tanya and Beauchard hoe young watermelons in the hot
humid heat. Beauchard's skin has turned from prison
pallor to tan, but it's apparent that he's still not in the best
health. Beauchard starts coughing, and when he can't
stop, Tanya hands him a jar of water.

                         TANYA
              Mr. Beauchard, you really ought to
              have Dr. York look at you.

                      BEAUCHARD
              Don't worry about me. Worry
              about the melons.

                         TANYA
              They look good. I don't know how
              I managed without you. As soon as
              I sell the cattle, I'll pay you.

                      BEAUCHARD
              Room and board's fine for now.

They look up as a wagon with GEORGE LANCHOR and his
five-year old daughter, JULIE, approach.

                         TANYA
              It's Mr. Lanchor and Julie.

GEORGE LANCHOR reins the wagon to the edge of the
field. It's piled high with household goods. Julie holds a
doll. Tanya walks to the wagon.

                      LANCHOR
              Hello, Tanya.

                         TANYA
              Hey, Mr. Lanchor.

Lanchor and Beauchard exchange nods.

                    TANYA
          Hi, Julie. My what a pretty doll.

                    JULIE
          Her name's Mimsey. You want to
          hold her, Tanya?

                    TANYA
          Sure, let me hold the baby.

Julie hands the doll to Tanya.

                    TANYA
          Looks like you're packing your
          whole house.

                    LANCHOR
          Julie and I are headed back East.
          Since her mother died there's been
          no one to look after her proper. My
          wife's family in Iowa are going to help
          out.
                    (beat)
          What about you young'n? Don't you
          have some family you can go to?

Tanya shakes her head.

                    LANCHOR
          You shouldn't go through another
          winter out here by yourself.

                    TANYA
          After the melons come in. I'll
          decide then.

                    LANCHOR
          We best be going. I hope to make
          Parsons by sundown. If night
          catches us we'll have to make do
          at the Bender Inn.

Beauchard looks up from rolling a cigarette.

                    TANYA
          I hope things work for you in Iowa.
                    (hands doll to Julie)
          Take good care of your dollie.

                LANCHOR AND JULIE
          Bye Tanya.

The Lanchors drive away.

                    BEAUCHARD
          Who are the Benders?

                    TANYA
          German innkeepers along the
          Osage. You met two of them in
          town. Kate and her brother.

                    BEAUCHARD
          The hellcat girl and the idiot in front
          of the hotel?

                         TANYA
                That's the ones.

Tanya turns back to work as Beauchard smokes his
cigarette.

                                        CUT TO:

EXT. BENDER INN - NIGHT

The Lanchor wagon stops in front of the inn. Kate Bender
appears in the lighted doorway.

                                        CUT TO:

INT. BENDER INN - NIGHT

Lanchor sits at the table, his back to the canvass curtain.
Kate sits across from him animatedly talking, offering him
more food. Little Julie Lanchor sleeps in a chair across the
room. John Bender strolls about the cabin, while Old
Woman Bender cooks over the stove. Old Man Bender
rises from his chair and walks behind the canvass. Kate
smiles beguilingly at Lanchor as Old Man Bender casts a
shadow wielding a hammer.

Lanchor is struck from behind. The Benders cluster around
his body, open a trap door under the table and shove
Lanchor into the cellar. Julie Lanchor awakes and
SCREAMS as Kate Bender walks toward the little girl.

                                        DISSOLVE TO:

INT. MC CLELLAND HOMESTAED - NIGHT

SCREAMS FROM THE PREVIOUS SCENE CARRY OVER.
Tanya, tears streaming down her face, sits up on the sofa
where she has fallen asleep reading a book. Beauchard
bursts into the house, his revolver drawn. Seeing no one,
he holsters the weapon and kneels beside Tanya.

                    BEAUCHARD
          What's wrong?

Tanya wraps her arms around Beauchard's neck.

                    TANYA
          It's raining.

                    BEAUCHARD
          It's not raining, kid.

                    TANYA
          It was in my dream... it was so
          real! Just like the night Papa died.

                    BEAUCHARD
               (gently strokes her hair)
          Talk to me.

                    TANYA
          Papa hadn't been well since the war.
          He was out chopping wood all day in
          the rain. Right after he came back in
          the wagon, he took sick. He was

                    TANYA
                    (cont'd)
          delirious. Over and over he kept
          trying to tell me something. I
          couldn't understand.

Abruptly Tanya lets go of Beauchard, embarrassed. She
stands and walks to a mantle and takes down the silver
sword that hangs overhead.

                    TANYA
          This was my father's. Victor Gregory
          McClelland.

Tanya hands the sword to Beauchard. He examines the
engraved sword, almost caressing it. Tanya watches
curiously as Beauchard steps back and with one smooth
quick motion, draws the sword from its sheath. The
CLASHING METALLIC SOUND and the wide arc created by
the sword is startling within the confines of the house.

                    TANYA
          My, you've done that before.

Beauchard sheathes the sword and replaces it over the
mantle.

                    BEAUCHARD
          Old battles best forgotten.

Tanya quickly moves to a piano which she taps on the side.
A hidden door opens and reaching inside, she removes a
revolver. She hands the gun to Beauchard.

                    BEAUCHARD
                    (surprised)
          It's a Lemat!

                      TANYA
          It was given to Papa when he
          joined the army.
                      (laughs)
          No coyotes going to get me.

Beauchard laughs and hands the gun back. Tanya returns
the gun to its hiding place and closes the hidden door. She
sits at the piano, the sad look returning to her face.

                      TANYA
          Do you ever see your family?

                    BEAUCHARD
                    (quietly)
          They're dead.

                      TANYA
          All of them?

                    BEAUCHARD
          All who were close. My father and
          two younger brothers died in the war.

                      TANYA
          What about your mother?

                    BEAUCHARD
          She was killed in the shelling of Atlanta.

TANYA
I'm sorry... my three older brothers
were killed in the war.
(beat)
It was the Kansas prairie that
killed my mother and father.
(beat)
Locusts and prairie fires in the
summer. Hunger and cold in the winter.

Beauchard sits beside Tanya on the piano bench

BEAUCHARD
Why do you stay?

Tanya's fingers move across the piano keys.

TANYA
(singing)
"We do not live, but only stay. And
are too poor to get away."

BEAUCHARD
(smiling)
You'll find your pot of gold.

TANYA
(looking at him closely)
Why did you say that?

BEAUCHARD
A figure of speech.

TANYA

Only gold around here is shaped like
a longhorn or a melon.

BEAUCHARD
(standing)

Speaking of which. It's time we got
some sleep.
(walking to the door)
Will you be all right?

TANYA

I believe so. Thank you.

BEAUCHARD

Think nothing of it ... good night.

TANYA
(staring after him)
(softly)

Good night... Beau.

EXT. MC CLELLAND HOMESTEAD - DAY

Tanya searches the farm.

TANYA
(shouts)

Mr. Beauchard? Mr. Beauchard?
Time for work.

INT. BARN - DAY

Tanya checks the barn, still unable to find Beauchard. In a corner are various garden implements (excluding a shovel). Tanya picks up a hoe.

CUT TO:

EXT. WATERMELON FIELD - DAY

Tanya works alone in the field.

TIME LAPSE

The sun beats down as Tanya continues to work. There is the SOUND OF GUNFIRE, followed by HORSES NEIGHING and CATTLE BELLOWING. Tanya turns around and sees Cutler's men on horseback, driving her cattle away.

Carrying the hoe, Tanya runs through the field after them. She runs until she collapses on the ground. Dazed, she watches the men and cattle disappear.

CLOSE SHOT

A man's boots. Tanya crawls backwards, until she sees that it's Beauchard. He helps her stand.

                    TANYA
          We've got to go after them. They stole
          my herd!

Tanya runs toward her horse. Beauchard grabs her.

45

                    BEAUCHARD
          You little fool, you can't go after
          them. They'll kill you.

                    TANYA
          I've got to get my cattle!

                    BEAUCHARD
          Cattle aren't worth your life. Let
          the sheriff handle it.

Beauchard pulls her to him and holds Tanya. She allows
him to comfort her for a moment, then abruptly jerks free.

                    TANYA
          Where have you been?

Beauchard doesn't respond. Tanya now sees that he's
covered with mud.

                    TANYA
          You've been gone all day. Where
          were you when I needed you?

                    BEAUCHARD
          I went hiking this morning and got
          lost in the woods. When I heard the
          gunfire, I followed the sound.

Tanya scoffs, picks up the hoe and walks toward the barn.

                                        CUT TO:

46

INT. BARN - DAY

Tanya replaces the hoe and sees that now there is a mud-covered shovel where before there was none. She looks out the barn door and watches Beauchard working in the field.

CUT TO:

EXT. MC CLELLAND HOMESTEAD - DAY

Tanya sits wearily on the steps while TWO FURNITURE MOVERS load her piano into a wagon. Beauchard walks in from the field, exhausted and dirty. His pace quickens when he sees the Furniture Movers.

                    BEAUCHARD
                    (to Tanya)
          Where are they going with your piano?

Tanya looks at the ground.

                    BEAUCHARD
                    (to Movers)
          Where are you taking the piano?

                    FIRST FURNITURE MOVER
          To town. That's if it's okay with you!

                    BEAUCHARD
          Well it's not.

47

SECOND FURNITURE MOVER
Listen, the little girl sold this piano to
Mr. Fibbs at Fibbs Furniture. We've got
orders to move it.

BEAUCHARD
(to Tanya)
Why did you sell it?

TANYA
I need the money.

BEAUCHARD
Certainly not enough to sell your
mother's piano.
(opening his wallet)
How much?

TANYA
Twenty dollars.

BEAUCHARD
(to First Mover)
Here's twenty. Tell Mr. Fibbs that
Miss McClelland changed her mind.

FIRST FURNITURE MOVER
Wait a minute. We went to a lot of
trouble coming out here and moving
this thing.

                    BEAUCHARD
        (with a sour look, handing Mover another bill)
                    Move it back!

The Furniture Movers shrug and move the piano back
inside.

                      TANYA
            (looking at Beauchard gratefully)
            Why'd you do that?

                    BEAUCHARD
            I got lucky. A lady in town bought a
            couple of my sketches. Besides, a
            child should never part with her
            mother's piano.
                      (beat)
            Don't you.

                                            CUT TO:

EXT. OSAGE TRAIL - DAY

With his horse tied behind the wagon, Beauchard drives
while Tanya reads one of her dime novels. She looks up as
the wagon slows. Nearby, along the side of the road, from
a tall desolate tree, dangles a man, hung by the neck. A
group of VIGILANTES, bandanas across their faces, and
armed with weapons, stand or sit on horseback. Tanya
looks away, covering her eyes. There is an apathetic look
on Beauchard's face. The Vigilantes wave them on.

                    BEAUCHARD
                      (cold)
          Vigilante justice.

ANGLE ON

Tanya shivers before adjusting her faded blue bonnet.

                                          CUT TO:

INT. SHERIFF'S OFFICE - DAY

Tanya stands before the SHERIFF seated at his desk.

                    SHERIFF
          Miss McClelland, I'm sorry there's
          no trace of your cattle. I tell you,
          I'm as puzzled about your herd being
          stolen as I am about all these missing
          people.

                    TANYA
          Who's missing?

                    SHERIFF
          More than a dozen people traveling
          through this area. They get to these
          parts, then they're never heard from
          again.
                      (beat)

SHERIFF
(cont'd)
This morning I received a wire from
George Lanchor's sister-in-law.
George and his little girl never made
it to Iowa.

TANYA
They've been gone for weeks.

SHERIFF
The same people who are responsible
for these missing folks could be the
ones who stole your cattle. You be
careful.

TANYA
I'll be all right. There's a hand
working at my place now.

SHERIFF
Who is he?

TANYA
William Beauchard.

SHERIFF
Where's he from?

TANYA
Georgia.

SHERIFF
You know anything else about him?

TANYA
He's a hard-working man, Sheriff.

SHERIFF
Wouldn't you be safer in town?

TANYA
(heading to the doorway)
I believe Mr. Beauchard to be an
honorable man. Please let me know
if you locate my cattle.

CUT TO:

EXT. TOWN MAIN STREET - DAY

A banner strung across the street reads "SETTLERS DAY".
Tanya browses the various booths that line the street filled
with TOWNS PEOPLE.

Beauchard walks out of the barber shop, completely
transformed. His hair has been cut short and beard
shaven. He stands for a moment watching Tanya, rubbing
his clean-shaven chin.

Tanya feels his gaze and turns. Momentarily she doesn't
recognize him. She becomes shy as she realizes that the
handsome man staring at her is Beauchard. He walks to
her.

BEAUCHARD
What do you think?

TANYA
I think ... you look ... dashing.

Beauchard smiles. Taking her hand, he leads Tanya down the sidewalk. Cindy and Lucy Watts, fashionably dressed as before, approach from the opposite direction. They eye Beauchard with interest.

CINDY WATTS
Find yourself a gunslinger, Tanya?

LUCY WATTS
A handsome one too. My, my
what will James Warren think?

CINDY WATTS
(giggles)
Poor, poor, James Warren.

LUCY WATTS
(singsong)
Tanya's got a gunslinger. Tanya's
got a gunslinger.

CINDY WATTS
Sister Lucy, I think we should go
comfort Mr. Warren in his time of need.

                    TANYA
          How'd you two snots like your
          curls dunked in the mud?

                  LUCY WATTS
          Why Tanya. Is that how a
          Southern girl talks?

                  CINDY WATTS
          It is for one who has no breeding.

Tanya grabs Cindy Watts by the hair and yanks her to a
horse trough and dunks Cindy's head into the water.

                  LUCY WATTS
          You're plain common, Tanya
          McClelland. Just like all Southerners.

Tanya picks up a large handful of mud from the street and
throws it in Lucy's face.

                    TANYA
          You're the common ones.

Towns People laugh. Amused, Beauchard pulls Tanya's
bonnet down over her eyes.

                  BEAUCHARD
          Come on, kid.

Beauchard leads Tanya to the wagon. He helps Tanya into
the wagon and climbs in.

                    BEAUCHARD
You ought to be enjoying yourself
instead of getting into fights. What
would your mother have said?

                     TANYA
                    (sullen)
No doubt something that would
make me ashamed.

As they drive by, the mud and water drenched Watts
sisters console each other. Tanya remains solemn, but
once past checks to see Beauchard isn't looking, then
turning around sticks her tongue out at the two sisters.
Tanya then scoots close to Beauchard and links her arm
through his.

                    BEAUCHARD
Where do your friends live?

                     TANYA
Two blocks down on the left.
There's plenty of time before the
dance, can't we get something to ...

                   CUTLER (V.O.)
Whoa, there!

Cutler and his Three Henchmen on horseback block the
road, their hands rest conspicuously on their holstered
guns.

                    CUTLER
          I want to talk to you, Beauchard.

                    TANYA
          Who is he?

Beauchard disengages his arm from Tanya and hands her
the reins.

                  BEAUCHARD
          Go to your friend's house.

Beauchard climbs from the wagon and unties his horse.

                    TANYA
          Beau, I don't like ...

                  BEAUCHARD
          This isn't about what you like. Do
          as I say! I'll meet you at the dance.
          Now drive!

Tanya glances from Beauchard to Cutler and back to
Beauchard.

                    TANYA
                  (to horse)
          Giddy up!

                                              CUT TO:

EXT. RAILROAD STATION - US.S. SENATOR SAMUEL
POMEROY'S PRIVATE RAILROAD CAR - DAY

Beauchard, Cutler and the Three Henchmen get off their horses. Cutler's men roughly direct Beauchard to the railroad car.

CUT TO:

INT. SENATOR POMEROY'S RAILROAD CAR - DAY

                    CUTLER
                 (to Beauchard)
               Mind your manners.

Beauchard eyes the splendid railroad car and the THREE WOMEN sipping champagne. SENATOR SAMUEL POMEROY, a gray-haired man in his sixties, enters. He is the epitome of the privileged politician of the time.

               SENATOR POMEROY
           Mr. Beauchard, welcome!

                  BEAUCHARD
         You appear to have the advantage.

               SENATOR POMEROY
               (offering his hand)
           Pomeroy. Samuel C. Pomeroy.

                  BEAUCHARD
         (ignoring the outstretched hand)
             As in Senator Pomeroy?

               SENATOR POMEROY
       I'm delighted you recognize my name.

                    BEAUCHARD
          I read a newspaper or two in
          Leavenworth... concerning your dealings.

                  SENATOR POMEROY
          Have a seat. Cigar?

                    BEAUCHARD
          As long as you're buying.

                  SENATOR POMEROY
          (signals a Woman to pour drinks)
          I trust your stay in the community
          has been pleasant.

                    BEAUCHARD
          It's had its moments.

The Woman hands Beauchard a drink which Beauchard
swirls under his nose before tasting.

                    BEAUCHARD
          Not bad.

                  SENATOR POMEROY
          As a member of the United States
          Senate, I've become accustomed to
          many fine things.
          (lifting his glass toward the Women)

BEAUCHARD
(watching Pomeroy for a reaction)
You're also a man accustomed to
getting what he wants. So far my stay
here hasn't been productive, but I
assure you before long I'm going to
get results concerning your gold.

SENATOR POMEROY
Naturally, as an elected official of
this state I'm concerned about the
whereabouts of any missing gold
shipment.
(laughs)
Especially when it happens to be a
token of appreciation for granting land
offices in certain Kansas towns.
Nevertheless, it's hardly foremost in
my mind.

BEAUCHARD
Then why am I here?

SENATOR POMEROY
The congressional convention meets
next week in Topeka. While I'm
practically assured of re-election, I do
hate to leave such matters to chance.

BEAUCHARD
I bet you do.

Cutler comes to attention. Beauchard smirks at Cutler.

                    SENATOR POMEROY
                  (laughs good-humoredly)
          I dislike leaving anything to chance.
          A certain state senator from this
          county, a man of considerable
          influence, a man by the name of
          Colonel Alexander York, is of particular
          interest to me.

Beauchard's hand shakes as he takes a long sip of his drink.

                    SENATOR POMEROY
          I understand you and Colonel York
          served in the same regiment during
          the war.

                    BEAUCHARD
          You do your homework, Senator.

                    SENATOR POMEROY
                  (smiling with the compliment)
          I want you to arrange a meeting
          between Colonel York and myself. In
          order to convince him to support my
          re-election.

                    BEAUCHARD
          You got me out of prison. Why not have
          me do what I do best?

SENATOR POMEROY
The way your hands shake?
(laughs)
Perhaps later. Right now, you're more
use to me as a link between York and
myself.

BEAUCHARD
What makes you think I won't blow
the whistle on you?

SENATOR POMEROY
You? A former convict? I suggest
you make use of your relationship
with Colonel York as a former comrade
in arms.
(pulls a roll of money from a
   drawer and hands it to Beauchard)
It can be profitable.

BEAUCHARD
(thumbing through the stack of money)
I'd think conspiracy to commit fraud
would bring a higher price.

SENATOR POMEROY
Don't overstep yourself, Beauchard.
Remember prison is easier to get
into than out of.

BEAUCHARD
(pocketing the money)
Say no more. I'll have York in Topeka.

SENATOR POMEROY
I'm glad we understand one another.

Beauchard stands, finishes his drink and hands the glass to Cutler as he walks to the door. Cutler angrily thrusts the glass into the hands of a Henchman.

CUTLER
You're taking your time finding
that gold. What's the hold up?

BEAUCHARD
The trouble with you, Cutler... you're
not patient.

CUTLER
Find that gold soon or that little
girl's gonna lose more than her cattle.
Or maybe you handled that already.

Beauchard strikes Cutler on the chin hard, knocking Cutler to the floor. Cutler leaps to his feet, ready to fight.

SENATOR POMEROY
Enough!

BEAUCHARD
(gives Cutler a hard look, then nods to Pomeroy)
See you in Topeka, Senator.

Beauchard walks out. Cutler's anger is apparent.

SENATOR POMEROY
Patience, Cutler. Patience.

CUT TO:

INT. SCHOOL HOUSE - NIGHT

TOWNS PEOPLE crowd the school house for the Settler's
Day Dance. A BAND plays popular music of the day for the
DANCERS.

Kate Bender is there surrounded by Towns Men. Cindy
Watts and Lucy Watts avoid Tanya, who's been
transformed by an upswept hair style and a billowing party
dress. Tanya stands with James Warren and MRS. YORK.

ANOTHER ANGLE

Colonel York and Dr. York discuss politics with Towns Men.

FIRST TOWNS MAN
Senator Pomeroy must be stopped.
He's destroying the good name of Kansas!

SECOND TOWNS MAN
He's lined his pockets with the fruits of
corruption for too long.

COLONEL YORK
Gentlemen, when I attend the
state convention, I have every
intention of voicing your grievances.

THIRD TOWNS MAN
There's talk that Pomeroy has the convention sewed up.

FOURTH TOWNS MAN
Don't be too hasty. My sister in Topeka says Senator Pomeroy donated a thousand dollars to her church.

FIFTH TOWNS MAN
I know for a fact that he donated two-thousand dollars to the Home For Destitute Children.

COLONEL YORK
There's no denying the Senator has made some hefty contributions, but the arm of his corruption far exceeds his generosity.

DR. YORK
Pomeroy has obtained his election through bribes and blackmail. His blatant disregard for the law cannot be allowed to continue.

TOWNS MEN ONE, TWO & THREE
That's right!

FIRST TOWNS MAN
Pomeroy's behavior is treasonous. We're behind you Colonel York.

COLONEL YORK
Thank you, gentlemen. Remember,
nothing is certain until the final ballot.
United we can stop Pomeroy.

ANOTHER ANGLE

James Warren gazes at Tanya, who is watching the front
door.

JAMES WARREN
Would you like to dance, Tanya?

TANYA
Not now, James.

COLONEL YORK (V.O.)
James, join us. There's someone I'd
like you to meet.

JAMES WARREN
(to Tanya)
I'll be right back.

James reluctantly joins Colonel York.

MRS. YORK
(to Tanya)
You look lovely in your mother's
dress, dear.

TANYA

Thank you, Mrs. York. You're very
kind.

MRS. YORK

The Colonel and I want to help you
in any way we can. It's a tragedy for
someone as young as yourself to lose
both her parents.

TANYA

When my parents and I moved here
you and Colonel York were the only
people who were civil to us.

MRS. YORK

Remember we're always here for you.
Now, I think it's time we concentrated
on having a good time. Will your
young man be here soon?

TANYA

I'm sure he'll be here any moment.

MRS. YORK

I hope he's worthy of you.
(beat)
The Colonel and I are very fond of James.

TANYA

There's Beau.

ANGLE ON DOORWAY

Tanya waves to Beauchard as he enters the room.
Beauchard nods and walks toward the two women. Mrs.
York eyes Tanya's "young man" skeptically.

                    TANYA
          I thought you'd never get here.
          You didn't have any problems did you?

                    BEAUCHARD
          No. No problems.

                    TANYA
          Mrs. York, may I present Mr. William
          Beauchard. Beau, this is Mrs. York.

                    BEAUCHARD
          How do you do, Ma'am.

                    MRS. YORK
          The Colonel and I have been looking
          forward to meeting you. Tanya's
          told us how much help you've been
          to her.

                    BEAUCHARD
          Thank you, Ma'am.

                    MRS. YORK
          Oh, look. Here comes the Colonel
          and James Warren now.

                        BEAUCHARD
                        (to Tanya)
Let's dance.

                        TANYA
Oh, I'd love to, but you haven't
met the Colonel.

                        BEAUCHARD
That can wait.
                   (bowing to Mrs. York)
Excuse us, Ma'am.

Beauchard leads Tanya to the dance floor as Colonel York
and James Warren join Mrs. York. Colonel York's face
grows stern when he sees Beauchard with Tanya.

ANOTHER ANGLE - DANCE FLOOR

It's apparent as Tanya and Beauchard dance that Tanya is
having the time of her life. She doesn't take her eyes off
Beauchard.

ANOTHER ANGLE - Kate Bender watches Beauchard,
dancing with Tanya, her interest in him kindled.

                        BEAUCHARD
Pretty dress. Pretty girl.

                        TANYA
Thank you.... you're a wonderful
dancer.

                    BEAUCHARD
          Say, do you think we could leave early?

                      TANYA
          Oh?

                    BEAUCHARD
          Like after this dance.

                      TANYA
          Beau!

                    BEAUCHARD
          Stop calling me that!

                      TANYA
          It fits you so. Especially since
          people now can see that dimple
          in your chin.

                    BEAUCHARD
              (laughing against his will)
                    (beat)
          Seriously. We've got a lot of work to do
          tomorrow.

The MUSIC STOPS. Tanya leads Beauchard from the dance
floor. He follows reluctantly.

                      TANYA
          First you have to meet Colonel York.
          I insist.

Tanya and Beauchard join the Yorks and James Warren.
The dislike on James' face is nearly as great as that of
Colonel York's.

                    TANYA
        Colonel York, I'd like you to meet...

                  BEAUCHARD
              (stretching out his hand)
        Hello, Alexander.

                COLONEL YORK
      (ignoring Beauchard's outstretched hand)
          I was fearful that the William
        Beauchard that Tanya spoke of was you.

                    TANYA
                  (uneasy)
        I had no idea you two gentlemen
        knew each other.

                COLONEL YORK
        Bogus Beauchard is no gentleman.

                  BEAUCHARD
        That was a long time ago, Alexander.

                COLONEL YORK
        Not long enough for a man who
        betrayed his country.

                    BEAUCHARD
          I had a trade that was in demand....
          by the Confederacy and the Union.

                    COLONEL YORK
          A trade! You were nothing but a
          profiteer! At the expense of your
          country.

                    BEAUCHARD
          The war made liars of us all. I've paid
          years for what I did.

                    COLONEL YORK
          You should have been shot as a
          traitor.

The nearby dancers react to the verbal hostility.

                    BEAUCHARD
          Think we might continue this
          conversation elsewhere, Alex?

                    COLONEL YORK
          Only at gun point.

Tanya steps in between the two men.

                    TANYA
          Beau, I'd like to dance.

                    BEAUCHARD
          I'd prefer a drink!

Beauchard strides to the food and drink table. Tanya starts to follow, but Colonel York stops her.

                    COLONEL YORK
          You're better without him.

ANOTHER ANGLE

Kate Bender detaches herself from the throng of Towns Men surrounding her and approaches a whiskey drinking Beauchard.

                    KATE BENDER
          Well, well. If it isn't the pea picker.

                    BEAUCHARD
          (glancing at Kate from head to toe)
          Well, well. If it isn't the serving wench.

Kate's eyes darken, then good-naturedly she utters a hearty laugh. She returns Beauchard's appraising stare.

                    KATE BENDER
          I hardly recognized you, now that
          the pea picker looks more like a prince.

                    BEAUCHARD
          I'm glad I meet with your approval, Kate.

                    KATE BENDER
          Let's see if your dancing meets with my
          approval.

Beauchard bows and leads Kate to the dance floor.

ANOTHER ANGLE

Tanya stares at Kate and Beauchard. She turns to flee the room, but is stopped by James Warren, who leads her to the dance floor. Tanya is unable to resist glancing at Beauchard and Kate throughout the dance. Her poker face barely hides her agony when Beauchard leads Kate outside.

EXT. SCHOOL HOUSE - NIGHT

Tanya walks outside and sees Beauchard kissing Kate Bender. She utters a gasp. Beauchard lets go of Kate. When Kate keeps her arms around him, Beauchard moves away and walks toward Tanya.

                    TANYA
          Stay away from me. You, you
          ... hypocrite!

Beauchard stares at her. James Warren walks outside.

                    TANYA
          How do you know Colonel York?

                    BEAUCHARD
          We served in the same regiment
          during the war.

                    TANYA
          Colonel York fought for the North.
          You fought for the South.

                    BEAUCHARD
          I never said that.

                      TANYA
          You lied.

                  JAMES WARREN
          Tanya, would you like me to take
          you home?

                      TANYA
          Would you please, James.
                    (to Beauchard)
          I'll leave the wagon.

Tanya gives Kate Bender a malicious look.

                      TANYA
          I'm sure you'll need it.

Tanya brushes past Beauchard, followed by James Warren.
Kate Bender walks up behind Beauchard.

                   KATE BENDER
          My, she certainly has a bee in her
          bonnet.
                     (beat)
          That's no reason to spoil our good
          time. Drive me home.

EXT. WOODS - NIGHT

CULT WORSHIPPERS dance around a large bonfire.
Beauchard leans against a tree, drinking from a whiskey

flask. He watches as Kate Bender seductively dances around the fire. The BEAT OF A DRUM grows louder. Abruptly, Kate stops dancing and walks to a tree stump where she picks up a hatchet and raises it high above her head.

CLOSE SHOT - Beauchard's face. His eyes grow large, reflecting the light of the bonfire. There is the SOUND OF A LOUD SQUEAL. Beauchard closes his eyes.

CUT TO:

EXT. BENDER INN - NIGHT

A lantern lights the inn as Beauchard and Kate pull up in the wagon. There is an eeriness about the place that makes Beauchard pause before helping Kate from the wagon. She leans against him, but Beauchard steps unsteadily backwards.

KATE BENDER
What's the matter? You sweet on that McClelland girl?

BEAUCHARD
(taking a drink from the whiskey flask)
What's it to you?

KATE BENDER
(running her fingers down his chest)
Nothing at all. Except, ... a lot of people think there's gold buried on McClelland land.... lots of gold.

BEAUCHARD
What makes them think that?

KATE BENDER
A year ago, a man was captured near
the McClelland farm. He'd stolen two
hundred fifty thousand dollars in gold. It's
never been found.

BEAUCHARD
Just because they found him near
there doesn't prove a thing. He could
have hidden it anywhere.

KATE BENDER
He didn't.

BEAUCHARD
How can you be sure?

KATE BENDER
(running her fingers across
the palm of Beauchard's hand)
I'm a spiritualist. I'm attuned to such
matters.

BEAUCHARD
(laughs)
Yeah, I saw your spirits tonight.
Come on, Kate. How do you really
know.

                    KATE BENDER
          That man stopped here. When he
          did, he had the gold with him.

                    BEAUCHARD
          You saw it?

                    KATE BENDER
          No, but the saddle bags were full
          and he wouldn't let anyone near them
          .... the McClelland place isn't so far.

                    BEAUCHARD
          If the kid had the gold, she'd be
          long gone.

                    KATE BENDER
          She might know something.

                    BEAUCHARD
          (nods, sipping from the whiskey flask)
          What should we do?

                    KATE BENDER
          With the exception of tonight, it's
          obvious that you've got her wrapped
          around your little finger.
                    (beat)
          Press her for information.

                    BEAUCHARD
          I want to press you.

ANOTHER ANGLE

Old Man Bender stands in the doorway.

> OLD MAN BENDER
> Daughter, is that you?

> KATE BENDER
> Yes, Pa.
> (to Beauchard)
> I better go in.

> BEAUCHARD
> (running a hand through his hair)
> Yeah, I better get back... and start
> pressin' for information.

They both laugh.

> KATE BENDER
> See you soon.

Beauchard climbs into the wagon and drives away. Kate walks into the house.

CUT TO:

INT. BENDER INN - NIGHT

Old Woman Bender sits in a rocking chair. Old Man Bender sits down in a chair. John Bender walks into the cabin. There is mud on his hands and boots. Kate looks contemptuously at all of them.

                         KATE BENDER
                  Was there any business tonight?

                         JOHN BENDER
                           (giggles)
                  Shore was.

John Bender nods toward the canvass curtain.

                         KATE BENDER
                         (disgusted)
                  Clean off your boots before you
                  track in more mud!
                           (beat)
                  I'm going to bed.

Kate walks behind the curtain.

INT. BEHIND CURTAIN - NIGHT

Kate lights a lantern. Cutler lies on a mattress. He reaches
for a cigar and lights it with the lantern.

                         CUTLER
                  You took your time gettin' home.

                                        CUT TO:

EXT. TARGET RANGE - DAY

Colonel York target practices with a revolver as Beauchard
drives up in the wagon. Beauchard watches as York

reloads. Holstering his gun, York then draws and fires six times at the target.

EXTREME CLOSE UP - All six shots are dead center. Colonel York turns and looks at Beauchard.

CUT TO:

EXT. OSAGE TRAIL - DAY

Riding along the trail, Tanya spots Beauchard's horse tied behind her wagon. She dismounts and ties her horse to a tree.

CUT TO:

EXT. VERDISGRIS RIVER – DAY

Tanya walks from behind a large tree and sees Beauchard, dirty and sweat drenched, knee-deep in a freshly dug hole. There are half a dozen similar holes nearby. A sneer appears on Tanya's face as she notices carvings in the bark of three blackjack oak trees.

Tanya pulls the heavy Lemat revolver from a holster and two-handed aims at Beauchard. He turns around when he hears her cock the gun.

TANYA
You're working mighty hard for a
hot summer day.

80

                    BEAUCHARD
          Put the gun down.

                    TANYA
          You no good dirty dog! You're
          looking for the gold.

                    BEAUCHARD
          (indicating the carvings on the trees)
          Thought I'd found it.

                    TANYA
          You and everybody else!

                    BEAUCHARD
          What does that mean?

                    TANYA
          Contrary to what people believe,
          there's no gold here. There never
          was. When word got out about the
          government agent, I found these
          trees. I dug half the night and for the
          next three days.

Beauchard climbs out of the hole. He sits down on the
ground and stares straight ahead, as if in shock.

                    TANYA
          I even have a map that my father
          drew for me the night he took sick.

BEAUCHARD

A map?

TANYA

Three trees with crows' feet carved
into them.

BEAUCHARD

A man named Janner told me I'd
find the gold buried within reach
of the tree roots. The trees with the
crows' feet carved into the bark.

TANYA

He must have been a liar, too. You
and your help and kind words! You
thought I could help you find the gold.

BEAUCHARD

Tanya, you know I genuinely like you.

TANYA

Poppycock!.... If there is any gold
here, it's mine. Do you hear me?
Mine!

BEAUCHARD

There'd be those who disagree.

Tanya fires the Lemat at a branch over Beauchard's head.
He dodges the tree limb as it falls.

                    BEAUCHARD
You little fool. Didn't anyone ever
tell you to be careful who you pull
a gun on?

                    TANYA
I bet you think I'm a fool. You and
that trollop Kate Bender. And those
men in town. I'd swear they're the
ones who stole my cattle.
                    (beat)
You're probably in with them. I want
your lying carcass off my land. Now!

                    BEAUCHARD
                (exhaling deeply)
All right. I'm going.

Beauchard stands using the shovel as a cane.

                    BEAUCHARD
You wouldn't shoot me in the
back, would you?

Beauchard turns to walk away. Abruptly, he spins around
and knocks the Lemat out of Tanya's hand with the shovel.
They fumble for the Lemat. Tanya reaches it first.
Beauchard twists her wrist.

                    TANYA
        Owwww!

Tanya tries to fire the gun, but Beauchard yanks it out of her hands. One-handed, he pins Tanya's arm behind her back.

                    TANYA
                  (yelling)
        Let me go!

Beauchard shoves her away. He holds the Lemat in the air, admiring it.

                    BEAUCHARD
              (twirling the Lemat)
        Cute little plaything.

                    TANYA
        Give me that. It was my father's gun.

                    BEAUCHARD
        So, you told me. Rebel officers were
        about the only people who had
        these. Don't see many Lemats
        around. No, siree.

                    TANYA
        What would you know about
        Confederate officers? .... Yankee!

                    BEAUCHARD
        Remember Miss McClelland, it was
        you who jumped to conclusions.

TANYA

You lyin', no good ...

Tanya lunges at Beauchard. He side-steps her, laughing.
Holding her at bay, one by one Beauchard fires off eight
more rounds. Into the air, clipping tree branches, and
lastly clumps of sage grass.

BEAUCHARD

A nine shooter. What a gun!

TANYA

Damn you.

BEAUCHARD

Temper, temper.
(handing back the gun)
Now are you sure you wouldn't
shoot me in the back?

Satisfied, Beauchard walks away. Tanya follows.

EXT. TRAIL - DAY

Beauchard mounts his horse and proceeds to roll a
cigarette one-handed as Tanya glares at him.

BEAUCHARD

Girl, I don't make excuses for what
I've done. Opportunity dangled itself
in front of me. I would have been a
fool not to stretch for it.
(beat)
The older a man gets, the harder it is

BEAUCHARD
(cont'd)
to face that he's alone and has little to
show for his life.

TANYA
I'm alone and don't have much of
anything. You don't see me doing
people dirt.

BEAUCHARD
Why don't you get married... to
someone like ... what's his name?
James? Yes, James would do nicely.
He'll look after you.
(stern)
Most of all you won't have to worry
where your next meal comes from.
Something you'll do if you stay here.

TANYA
James! He's milk toast. Why should I
settle for a half-life. You haven't.

BEAUCHARD
I had to settle for a lot less than I
bargained on, girl.

TANYA
What does that mean?

                    BEAUCHARD
        That means, I thought you were
        smarter.
                    (indicating the Lemat)
        Remember what I said about pointing
        that gun.
                    (doffing his hat)
        You all don't lose any sleep reloading
         that thing.
                    (laughs)

Beauchard rides away. Tanya clutches the Lemat in her
hands.

                    TANYA
                    (mumbles)
        As if I can afford powder and shot.
                    (shouts)
        I hate you! I hate you!
                    (quietly)
        Beau.

Tanya fumbles in her pocket for a handkerchief and blows
her nose. She kicks a clod of grass, looks in the direction
Beauchard has ridden, looks at the gun, then walks back
toward the woods.

                                              CUT TO:

EXT. TAFT HOTEL LOBBY - DAY

Beauchard sits sketching. Colonel York walks into the
hotel. Beauchard sees him and pockets the sketch.

COLONEL YORK
I'm ready.

Beauchard stands and walks up the stairs. Colonel York follows.

CUT TO:

INT. SENATOR POMEROY'S SUITE – NIGHT

There is a knock at the door. Cutler opens the door. He nods to Beauchard but stiffens when Beauchard hands his hat to Cutler. Colonel York follows Beauchard inside. Senator Pomeroy, casually dressed in a silk smoking jacket, shakes hands with Beauchard.

SENATOR POMEROY
Good to see you again, Beauchard.

BEAUCHARD
Senator Pomeroy ... Colonel
Alexander York. Alex, Senator Pomeroy.

The Senator and Colonel shake hands. Beauchard starts to sit down.

SENATOR POMEROY
That will be all, Beauchard.

Cutler tosses Beauchard his hat.

                    COLONEL YORK
                    (to Beauchard)
          Thanks, William. The Senator and
          I have a lot to discuss.

Beauchard puts on his hat, then nodding to Pomeroy and
Colonel York, walks out the door.

                                             CUT TO:

INT. STATE SENATE – DAY

Senator Pomeroy walks confidently into the chamber
packed with CONGRESSIONAL REPRESENTATIVES. He is
loudly applauded as he makes his way to his seat. The
majority of the Congressional Representatives appear
supportive of Pomeroy, while the look on the faces of some
clearly displays their dislike.

There is moderate applause as Colonel York makes his way
to the podium.

ANGLE ON - PODIUM

                    COLONEL YORK
          Mr. President and gentlemen of the
          convention, before I place any
          gentleman in nomination, I desire to
          make a statement. As it concerns all
          present and is of great importance to
          the state of Kansas, present and future,
          I request the careful attention of all
          members to what I say.

ANGLE ON - Senator Pomeroy smiles.

> COLONEL YORK
> Before I came to Topeka, the people
> of my district in both Wilson and
> Montgomery counties consulted
> what action I proposed to take in
> reference to Mr. Pomeroy. I told
> them that I believe both the best and
> highest interest of the state
> demanded the election of some other
> man than S.C. Pomeroy to the US Senate
> and pledge myself to work and vote
> against Mr. Pomeroy.

A murmur is heard among the Congressional
Representatives. Senator Pomeroy straightens in his chair,
the smile wiped from his face.

> COLONEL YORK
> I came with that determination and
> I cheerfully and enthusiastically align
> myself with the anti-Pomeroy element
> in the legislature, believing that in his
> defeat lay the rejuvenation of the state.

ANGLE ON
Congressional Representatives are bewildered and amazed
at Colonel York's speech.

ANGLE ON
Senator Pomeroy beckons an AIDE.

SENATOR POMEROY
Get him off the podium!

AIDE
Senator, he has the floor.

SENATOR POMEROY
I don't pay you for excuses.
Something's gone wrong. Terribly
wrong.

AIDE
I'll do what I can sir.

COLONEL YORK
This week I was asked to have a
private business interview with
Mr. Pomeroy. On Monday I was
received by Mr. Pomeroy in his private
room at the Taft House. At that
interview, in consideration of my
promising to vote for him in the joint
convention, he promised me twelve-
thousand dollars.

A LOUD MURMUR is heard throughout the chamber.

CONGRESSIONAL REPRESENATIVE
That's an outrage!

                    COLONEL YORK
        Seven thousand dollar which he paid
        that night and five thousand dollars I
        am to receive after I have voted for him.

ANGLE ON

SECOND and THIRD CONGRESSIONAL Representatives
flanked by Pomeroy's Aide.

            SECOND CONGRESSIONAL REPRESENTATIVE
                You're a liar! Senator Pomeroy would
                do no such thing.

            THIRD CONGRESSIONAL REPRESENTATIVE
                Get off the podium!

ANGLE ON

            FOURTH CONGRESSIONAL REPRESENTATIVE
                Quiet! Let him finish!

            FIFTH CONGRESSIONAL REPRESENTATIVE
                Pomeroy's capable of anything. Continue
                Colonel York.

                    COLONEL YORK
        I now in the presence of this honored
        body hand over the amount of seven
        thousand dollars, just as I received it
        and ask that it be counted by the
        secretary.

Colonel York hands a large parcel of money to a CLERK.

ANGLE ON
Pomeroy is furious.

CUT TO:

EXT. GENERAL STORE - DAY

Beauchard walks into the store.

INT. GENERAL STORE - DAY

Beauchard collects boxes of ammunition from the store's stockpile. As he presents his purchases to the STORE CLERK, his eyes rest on various farm implements, one which is a saw.

CUT TO:

EXT. GENERAL STORE – DAY

Beauchard leaves the store, carrying several large bundles which he packs into saddle bags. Beauchard adjusts the straps holding the rifle and shotgun. Then mounting his horse, Beauchard rides out of town.

CUT TO:

EXT. JAMES WARREN'S HOME - DAY

Tanya, dressed in her best, ties the horse drawn wagon to a hitching post. She climbs steps to the imposing house.

James Warren opens the front door and greets her.

CUT TO:

INT. STATE SENATE - DAY

> COLONEL YORK
> I went into Mr. Pomeroy's room
> with the purpose of unmasking one
> of the blackest criminals and most
> wicked men that ever-set foot upon the
> soil of Kansas. I intended to take his
> money should he offer it to me and
> expose him as I have done today. I do not
> deny that I deliberately deceived him. I
> told him that I would vote for him and I
> now redeem that pledge by voting for
> Samuel C. Pomeroy to be termed to the
> penitentiary for a term not less than
> twenty years!

As Colonel York ends his speech, the members of the convention break into LOUD CHEERS.

ANGLE ON

Senator Pomeroy sits with his head bowed.

CUT TO:

INT. JAMES WARREN'S HOME – DAY

Seated ramrod straight and sipping tea is Tanya in the drawing room with James Warren and MRS. WARREN,

James' staunch, disapproving mother. The strained silence is interrupted by a steady "tick tock" of a grandfather clock.

                    MRS. WARREN
          Miss McClelland, it grieves me to
          learn that you, a young girl, have
          opened yourself to gossip by hiring a
          bachelor ranch hand to live on the
          premises.

                    TANYA
               (clenching her fists)
          It was necessary for me to hire help,
          Mrs. Warren.

                    MRS. WARREN
          Unfortunate. Nevertheless, the
          circumstances are totally inappropriate.

                    JAMES WARREN
          Mother, I have urged Tanya to
          contemplate a sale of her homestead.

                    MRS. WARREN
          Who would purchase it? Local land
          is for the taking.

                    TANYA
          My homestead is good, fertile land.
          There's the house, barn ...

MRS. WARREN
And what would you do if you move
to town?

JAMES WARREN
(clears his throat)
Tanya and I have ... we've been ...
discussing the future.

MRS. WARREN
Really.

JAMES WARREN
Naturally, I ... Tanya and I... ah, ...
your blessing.

MRS. WARREN
(ice cold)
James, you are free to choose
whomever you wish to discuss the
future. Yet you must consider your
options. A political career is such an
expensive venture these days.

JAMES WARREN
There's my law practice.

MRS. WARREN
My point exactly. Similar interests
and life ambitions are of the utmost
importance in a personal relationship.
(to Tanya)

                    MRS. WARREN
                     (cont'd)
          How is your watermelon crop
          progressing, dear?

                      TANYA
          Splendidly.

                    MRS. WARREN
          James, did I mention that I saw Mrs.
          Watts and her two beautiful daughters at
          church this morning?

                   JAMES WARREN
          No, Mother.

                    MRS. WARREN
          That Lucy is such a young lady.
          Impeccable manners. Then Cindy is
          quite the fashion setter. She was
          wearing a dress straight from Paris.
          The three of them will be here for
          dinner this evening.

ANGLE ON

Tanya and James Warren

                   JAMES WARREN
          How delightful. Six for dinner.

Mrs. Warren's expression says, "No, more like five."

                    MRS. WARREN
          James, the fact of the matter is until
          your thirtieth birthday, young financial
          resources are entrusted to me.

Intimidated and torn, James Warren stalls in silence.

                    MRS. WARREN
          Five years, James.

                      TANYA
                    (standing)
          Mrs. Warren, thank you ever so
          much for tea. As always, it's been an
          indescribable pleasure.

James winches.

                      TANYA
          We shall have to do it again.
                    (beat)
          Say in the next century!

James' eyes open wide. Tanya gives a quick curtsy and
waltzes from the room.

                                              CUT TO:

EXT. JAMES WARREN'S HOME - DAY

Tanya is out the door when James reaches her.

                    JAMES WARREN
           Why did you do that? Mother would
           come around.

                         TANYA
           Spare me, James. Your mother will
           never come around where I'm
           concerned. And for you to utter not
           one word on my behalf...
                         (sighs)
           James, ... you're milk toast.

Tanya walks away.

                                          CUT TO:

INT. RUNDOWN HOTEL ROOM - DAY

Cutler reads a newspaper.

CLOSE SHOT: Headline: INGALLS 115, POMEROY 0.

Cutler slams down the paper. He straps on his gun belt and
walks out of the room, slamming the door behind him.

                                          CUT TO:

EXT. MC CLELLAND HOMESTEAD - CEMETERY - DAY

Tanya prunes the prairie grass that grows around the
tombstones. She looks up and sees Dr. York on horseback.

TANYA

Dr. York? Where are you off to?

DR. YORK

Fort Scott to see my father. He's
been ill.

TANYA

I'm sorry to hear that.
(beat)
I heard of Colonel York's success in
Topeka. It's a wonderful thing he's done.

DR. YORK

It's time Kansas was rid of that
scoundrel Pomeroy.

TANYA

When will the Colonel be home?

DR. YORK

In two weeks.
(beat)
The watermelons are about ready for harvest.

TANYA

Won't be long.

DR. YORK

Is that Beauchard fellow around?

TANYA

I haven't seen that no good skunk
for weeks. Why?

DR. YORK

Alexander writes that the "no good
skunk" as you call him was
instrumental in bringing about
Pomeroy's downfall.

TANYA

What?

DR. YORK

My brother says Beauchard was able
to convince Pomeroy that Alex would
go along with the bribe and vote for
him in the convention.

TANYA

I don't understand. Beau told me
his mother was killed during the
shelling of Atlanta. But, he fought
with Colonel York in the war!

DR. YORK

According to Alex, Beauchard's
mother was from Atlanta. She was
an artist. She met and fell in love with
Beauchard's father during a trip

                         DR. YORK
                         (cont'd)
          North. Mrs. Beauchard got across the
          line to be with her father before the
          battle of Atlanta. That's when she
          was killed.

                         TANYA
          Why was he in prison?

                         DR. YORK
          During the war, federal currency was
          counterfeited extensively. Some
          amongst the Confederacy thought
          it would lead to the economic
          collapse of the Union. Beauchard
          had the ability for meticulous
          attention to detail.
                         (beat)
          One that made him an expert
          counterfeiter.
                         (beat)
          I should be going. If you see
          Mister Beauchard, give him my regards.

                         TANYA
                         (numb)
          I will.

Dr. York rides away down the Osage Trail.

                                              CUT TO:

INT. TANYA'S HOUSE – DAY

Tanya is seated at the table. She spoons a small bowl of
mush out of a pot. She scrapes the bottom of a sugar bowl
and finds it empty. The SOUND OF A HORSE IS HEARD.
Tanya opens the door.

EXT. TANYA'S HOUSE - DAY

Beauchard's horse stands rider less. Tanya examines the
animal and finds it covered with dried blood.

                                                    CUT TO:

EXT. RAILROAD DEPOT - DAY

The Towns People have turned out for the arrival of the
train. Banners read, "WELCOME HOME SENATOR YORK".
Tanya wanders through the crowd. Mrs. York and TWO
YORK CHILDREN are on a raised platform. In the crowd,
Kate Bender stands next to her brother, John. Tanya and
Kate see one another, the dislike they feel, apparent.

ANOTHER ANGLE

The train arrives and Colonel York steps off the train onto
the platform. Towns People CHEER LOUDLY.

                        COLONEL YORK
                Ladies and gentlemen, thank you
                for your kind demonstration.
                Together we have triumphed
                over and shown the people of
                this nation that the good citizens

                            103

                    COLONEL YORK
                      (cont'd)
               of Kansas will not tolerate
               mercenary politicians.

The Towns People cheer. Cutler walks through the crowd
and stops next to Kate Bender. She speaks to him and
Cutler nods.

ANOTHER ANGLE

Colonel York steps from the platform, followed by Mrs.
York and York Children. Tanya waits for them.

                    COLONEL YORK
                    (to Mrs. York)
               I received your telegram. Has
               my brother returned?

                      MRS. YORK
               Nothing has been heard of
               Jonathan since he left your
               father's ten days ago.

                       TANYA
               Colonel York. Oh, Colonel York,
               I must speak to you.

                    COLONEL YORK
               What is it, Tanya?

                       TANYA
               Have you seen Mr. Beauchard?

                         104

COLONEL YORK
Not since before the convention.

TANYA
Two days ago, his horse came to
the farm, rider less and covered
with blood!

COLONEL YORK
Have you spoken with the sheriff?

TANYA
It was a waste of time. He was his
usual worthless self.

COLONEL YORK
Try not to worry. I'm going to get
some men together to search for
my brother. We'll look for
Beauchard also.

CUT TO:

EXT. MC CLELLAND HOMESTEAD - DAY

The house and barn are deserted. It is VERY QUIET.

CLOSE UP: The watermelon field. The watermelons are
ripe, ready for picking.

THE SOUND OF GUN FIRE IS HEARD.

CLOSE UP: The watermelons explode.

ANOTHER ANGLE

Edge of the woods. From behind a tree, Tanya watches
helplessly as Cutler and his Henchmen destroy the
watermelon field. Her fear turns to anger as they ride
away. Tanya runs to the barn and gets her horse. She
rides after Cutler and his Henchmen. Her bonnet dangles
by the ribbons around her neck.

                                                    CUT TO:

INT. BENDER INN - NIGHT

Kate Bender paces the room while the rest of her family
furiously packs whatever they can into travel bags. Cutler
strides into the cabin. He's amused at the Bender's frantic
behavior.

                    KATE BENDER
                      (screams)
            You must be crazy coming here!
            That holier-than-thou Colonel
            York was here this afternoon with
            a posse looking for his brother!

                    CUTLER
            So, what's the rush?

                    KATE BENDER
            I told York that his brother stopped
            for supper, then rode on. York

KATE BENDER
(cont'd)
pretended like he believed me. But
they'll be back. I know it!

CUTLER
I wish you were as sure about
Beauchard.

KATE BENDER
I tell you, he's dead! I finished the job.

CUTLER
Yeah, then how come his body
hasn't turned up?

KATE BENDER
His horse ran off with him. No man
could survive that gun blast. Now,
I've done my work for you! That
posse's out for blood. And we're
getting out of here. Now!

CUTLER'S HENCHMAN
Hey, boss!

Cutler and Kate look toward the door as the Henchman
walks in dragging Tanya behind him.

HENCHMAN
Look what I caught! Somebody
was following us. And look what
she's packing.

The Henchman holds up the Lemat. Tanya kicks him, he shoves her into the cabin. Tanya lands on the floor.

                    JOHN BENDER
          Look who dropped in to see us.
          Little Tanya McClelland.
                    (beat)
          Hey, Pa! Let's have a go at her.

Bender grapples with Tanya on the floor.

                    JOHN BENDER
          Better be good or you'll end up
          like your boyfriend.

                    TANYA
          What have you done with Beauchard?

                    JOHN BENDER
          Don't worry. We'll take on where
          he left off.

Tanya gives Bender a vicious kick in the groin. Bender reels with agony. Old Man Bender grabs for Tanya, tearing off her bonnet.

                    TANYA
          Give me that!

Tanya reaches for the bonnet. There is a RIPPING SOUND. A piece of paper floats to the floor.

KATE BENDER
What's that?

Kate grabs the paper, looks at it then hands the paper to Cutler.

CLOSE UP: A MAP. Two wavy lines representing the bend in a river border three crudely drawn trees, marked with sets of crows' feet. A large "X" is drawn across the trees.

ANGLE ON

Cutler and Kate are pleased.

CUT TO:

EXT. BENDER INN – DAY

A mixture of somber and angry Towns People are gathered around the deserted cabin that has been rolled off its foundation. The eeriness that has prevailed is still present.

ANOTHER ANGLE

A TRAVELER in a wagon carries a bloodied Beauchard. He climbs off the wagon, his left arm in a sling. Beauchard limps toward the crowd.

TOWNS WOMAN
The Benders always did give me the willies.

TOWNS MAN
Maudie Taylor claims she had to
hide in the hills all night when
the Benders tried to kill her.

Beauchard moves through the crowd to the cabin
foundation where he sees an open trap door leading to a
cellar. Beauchard recoils from a foul smell from the cellar.

SECOND TOWNS MAN
I wouldn't go down there if I was
you. The whole cellar's soaked
with blood. Human blood.

The Second Towns Man points toward the orchard where
Towns Men dig with hoes and shovels.

SECOND TOWNS MAN
A tunnel leads to the orchard.
There's graves out there. Lots
of 'em.

THIRD TOWNS MAN
Eight so far. Their heads smashed
and throats cut! The first one
found was Dr. York.

BEAUCHARD
Does Colonel York know about
his brother?

                    FIRST TOWNS MAN
          You bet he does. The Colonel is
          in Cherryvale gettin' a big posse
          to hunt down the Benders.

                    TOWNS WOMAN
          Colonel York won't let those
          murdering Benders get away
          with this.

Beauchard picks up an object from the floor. It is Tanya's
bonnet.

                    TOWNS MEN (O.S.)
          My lord. Here's another one!

The Towns People run to the orchard where several
Towns People stand, stone-faced or crying.

                    SECOND SEARCHER
          Those animals.

The Towns People stand frozen, a mixture of anger and
disbelief on their faces. Several curse, others mutter for
revenge. Towns Woman kneels next to the grave.

                    TOWNS WOMAN
                      (crying)
          It's a little girl!

The Towns Woman holds up Julie Lanchor's doll.
Beauchard stares at the doll. He looks at Tanya's bonnet

                          111

clutched in his hands. He strides to a Towns Man's horse and mounts it.

> TOWNS MAN
> Where the hell you think you're
> goin' with my horse?

> BEAUCHARD
> After the Benders. Tell Colonel
> York, Bogus said, "Get to the
> McClelland farm!"

Reining sharp, Beauchard spurs the horse to a gallop.

CUT TO:

EXT. WOODS ALONG RIVERBANK - DAY

The SOUND OF LOCUSTS IS LOUD. The humid summer heat is suffocating. Kate Bender shoves Tanya through the woods. They are followed by John Bender, Cutler and Two Henchmen, carrying shovels. All are hot, tired and cross, except John Bender who waves the Lemat in the air as he walks.

> JOHN BENDER
> (singsong)
> We're gonna be rich. We're gonna
> be rich.

> KATE BENDER
> Shut up, idiot!

Kate grabs the Lemat from John Bender.

> KATE BENDER
> (to Tanya)
> Where in blazes are we? We've
> been walking for hours.

> TANYA
> It can't be much further. It's so easy
> to get turned around in the woods.

> FIRST HENCHMAN
> Boss, she's leadin' us on a wild goose
> chase.

> CUTLER
> If she is, we'll drown her in the river.

Cutler and his Henchmen laugh. Tanya shudders. Kate
shoves her.

> KATE BENDER
> She's lying. If she'd found it, she'd
> be gone.

> TANYA
> I told you... I found the map the
> other day.

> CUTLER
> It could have been Beauchard's.

                    TANYA
                  (desperate)
          That's right! I stole it from him.
          That lousy, no good skunk. He
          wanted it for himself. I was going
          after it when I saw you in my
          watermelon field. Beauchard hid the
          map in my house. He must have
          been waiting for the right time to go
          and get the gold.

Kate and Cutler seem to accept her explanation.

                    TANYA
          Are all of you going to divvy up the gold?
          I mean, that's a lot of gold. But divided
          between how many people? Seven
          ... eight?

Tanya's questions have a disquieting effect on members of
the search party.

                    TANYA
                  (to Cutler)
          You know there's Kate and John,
          their folks, you, and your men.
                  (beat)
          That'd sure be a lot of gold for one
          person.

Kate's face contorts with anger. She pistol-whips Tanya
across the face. Tanya reels from the blow.

                    TANYA
        Ahh!

                  KATE BENDER
        Shut up!

                    CUTLER
        Lay off her! She's no good to us
        if you knock her out.

                  KATE BENDER
        If you hadn't been so all fired bent
        on gettin' York and his family, we
        wouldn't be in this mess.
                    (to Tanya)
        What's wrong with you?

Tanya stands perfectly still. She looks at Cutler.

                    TANYA
        There's your gold.

Tanya points toward the three blackjack oaks with the
carvings. She looks at the ground that is smooth and
undisturbed around the trees. Kate runs her hands over
the carvings on the trees, smiling.

                    CUTLER
        Get to diggin'!

John Bender and the Two Henchmen dig furiously in
between the trees.

                      115

CUTLER
Now, that's more like it. Okay, kid,
now for ...

Cutler turns around, but Tanya has vanished.

CUT TO:

EXT. DEEP WOODS - DAY

Tanya runs as fast as she is able through the deep brush.
Branches and thorns tear at her face, hair and clothing.
She is perspiration soaked, running for her life, falling
down, leaping to her feet, stumbling again. The SOUND of
LOUD CRASHING OF BRUSH behind her grows closer and
closer with every step she takes. Tanya slips on the moist
foliage and plummets down a steep embankment.

She is dazed. Crawling on hands and knees, Tanya hides
underneath thick brush as Kate Bender races past.
Catching her breath, Tanya gets up and runs in the
opposite direction. Right into Cutler.

CUTLER
What's your rush little girl?

CUT TO:

EXT. MC CLELLAND HOMESTEAD - DAY

Beauchard inches around the corner of the house. He
looks inside through a window.

116

MEDIUM SHOT - Window.

The inside of the house is in shambles. Old Woman Bender stuffs food into a traveling bag. Old Man Bender is seen pouring kerosene around the house.

ANGLE ON

Beauchard heads for the barn.

INTERIOR BARN

Beauchard enters and finds Third Henchman lying in a heap in the back of a stall. The man is dead.

Beauchard spins around, to the SOUND OF FOOTSTEPS, gun in hand. Old Man Bender walks into the barn carrying a shotgun. Old Woman Bender follows him. Beauchard leaps for cover, groaning as he lands on his bad arm. Old Man Bender levels the shotgun at Beauchard. Beauchard fires. There is a GUN BLAST and a flash of fire.

                                                    CUT TO:

EXT. WOODS

John Bender and Two Henchmen stand in holes they have dug. Cutler walks into the clearing dragging Tanya. Kate Bender follows holding the gun.

                        CUTLER
            Haven't you found the gold yet?

FIRST HENCHMAN
Nothing but dirt and rock, boss.
Did you hear the gunfire?

CUTLER
Yeah.

SECOND HENCHMAN
What do you make of it?

CUTLER
I'm not sure. Keep digging.

Kate and John Bender exchange looks that Cutler notices.

CUTLER
What's with you two?

KATE BENDER
(snaps)
Nothing!

CUTLER
Maybe you've got something
planned. Maybe you don't want to
share.

FIRST HENCHMAN
Look!

First Henchman points toward the top of the trees where
smoke is seen.

                              TANYA
             Fire.
                            (to Kate)
             You told them to burn the house!

                          KATE BENDER
             Now people will think you gave up
             and left.

                             CUTLER
             That was a fool thing to do. It'll draw
             attention.

                          JOHN BENDER
                            (to Kate)
             They weren't suppose to set the
             fire until we were ready to leave.

Tanya lunges at Kate. The two women roll across the
ground wrestling for the gun. First Tanya, then Kate gets
the better of the fight. ONE GUNSHOT, a SECOND
GUNSHOT, a THIRD GUNSHOT and a FOURTH GUNSHOT.

                             CUTLER
               Stop it. You're going to get us all
               killed you crazy ...

Cutler attempts to break up the two struggling women
when another GUN FIRES, the shot ripping the ground near
Cutler.

                    BEAUCHARD (V.O.)
            What's the matter, Cutler? Trouble
            in paradise?

ANOTHER ANGLE

Beauchard stands at the edge of the water with a gun
pointed directly at Cutler. A saddle bag is draped over his
right shoulder. Tanya wrenches the gun free from Kate
Bender.

                         TANYA
            Beau!

                       BEAUCHARD
                      (to Cutler)
            You've been busy. Is this what
            you're lookin' for?

Beauchard opens the saddle bag and pulls out a glistening
gold bar. The Benders, Cutler and his men stare, greed in
their eyes. As Beauchard replaces the gold, the First
Henchman goes for his gun. Beauchard fires his gun, killing
the man. Cutler draws his gun and fires as he dodges
behind a tree.

ANGLE ON

Second Henchman still in the dug hole fires. Beauchard
shoots him.

ANOTHER ANGLE

John Bender lunges for the gun Tanya holds. They struggle

                          120

and the GUN FIRES, killing Bender. Kate takes one look at her brother and runs.

ANGLE ON

BEAUCHARD
So much for your gold, Cutler.

Beauchard hurtles the saddle bag into the air. In SLOW MOTION the saddle bag falls through the air and into the river. Cutler dashes from behind the trees firing his gun and runs toward the river as the saddle bag disappears from sight. Beauchard fires twice, killing Cutler.

ANGLE ON

Tanya runs after Kate.

DEEP WOODS

Tanya pursues Kate up the riverbank

CUT TO:

EXT. MC CLELLAND HOMESTEAD - DAY

Tanya stops at the edge of the clearing, overwhelmed at the sight of the house and barn burning.

ANGLE ON

Kate Bender climbs into a wagon.

TANYA

Stop.

Kate grabs the reins and whips the horse into a run straight
toward Tanya. Tanya fires the gun until it clicks empty.
Kate reins the horse to a stop, her eyes glazed with craze.
She grabs a shovel from the wagon.

KATE BENDER

You're a lousy shot.
(maniac scream)

Kate lunges toward Tanya with the shovel. Tanya fumbles
with the Lemat's fire selector. As Kate swings the shovel
there is a SHOT GUN BLAST from the Lemat. Momentarily,
Kate's expression turns to one of confusion as she stares at
her blood-soaked body, before collapsing to the ground.

TANYA
(staring at the body)
Never underestimate a rebel.

The SOUND OF RIDERS ON HORSEBACK catches Tanya's
attention.

ANGLE ON

Colonel York's POSSE reins to a stop, all guns drawn.

CUT TO:

122

EXT. MC CLELLAND HOMESTEAD - SUNDOWN

The barn destroyed by fire. The nearby house and prairie charred.

ANGLE ON – CEMETERY

Tanya kneels by her parents' graves. She is dirty and her clothes are covered with soot. Colonel York stands behind her. Several Posse Members approach on horseback.

> FIRST POSSE MEMBER
> Everything's been tended to
> Colonel York. They're buried .... deep.

> SECOND POSSE MEMBER
> You ready to ride, Colonel?

> COLONEL YORK
> You men go on ahead. I'll be along
> shortly.

The Posse rides away.

> TANYA
> Where's Beau?

> COLONEL YORK
> Beauchard was serving federal time.
> He might have to go back to prison
> if attention were drawn to him.
> Pomeroy still has powerful friends in
> Washington.

TANYA

He's gone?

COLONEL YORK

The wanted posters the Governor
issued for the Benders will be posted.
It's best for everyone if the Benders
simply disappear off the face of the
earth... and Bogus Beauchard never
heard from again.
(beat)
We must put this behind us. I also
think it's time we laid the war to rest.

Tanya leans on her parents' headstones. Then slowly she
stands and looking to Colonel York, nods.

CUT TO:

EXT. YORK HOME – DAY

The York house is a neat, prosperous looking home,
surrounded by shrubbery. Tanya sits on the front porch
swing, attempting to read a dime novel. She stands, paces
the porch, then goes back to her book with a deep sigh.
Tanya continues to read until the SOUND OF A MAN
WHISTLING "DIXIE" is heard. She looks up as Beauchard
approaches, driving a buggy.

BEAUCHARD

I figured I'd find James Warren sitting
with you on the porch swing.

Tanya studies Beauchard's face. The corners of her mouth slowly turn upward.

                    TANYA
          I could never marry James Warren.
          I don't love him.

                    BEAUCHARD
          Wish I'd known your pa. He was a
          clever man.

                    TANYA
          Why do you say that?

                    BEAUCHARD
          He knew it'd look suspicious if an ex-
          Confederate officer suddenly came
          into a lot of money. He knew
          somebody was bound to come looking
          for the gold. It was hell of a search,
          but I finally found the trees your pa
          cut down. The ones with the stumps
          cut to ground level.
                    (beat)
          Right at the bend in the river where
          Janner told me. The oak trees Janner
          carved, ... not the ones your father
          carved as a decoy.

                    TANYA
          You threw the gold into the river.
          I saw you.

                    BEAUCHARD
                 (shaking his head)
           Kid, an old counterfeiter is full of
           tricks. Lordy, but I hated tossing
           that gold bar. However, we all must
           make sacrifices.

Beauchard opens two charred saddle bags to reveal a pile
of glistening gold bars.

                    BEAUCHARD
           I told you never to sell your piano.
           That trap door wasn't the only hiding
           place it had to offer.

Rising from the swing, Tanya tosses her book aside and
runs to Beauchard.

                                      DISSOLVE TO:

INT. MANSION LIBRARY - KANSAS CITY 1936 - NIGHT

                   WILLIAM (O.S.)
             Catching up on your reading?

ANGLE ON

The Elderly Woman sets the newspaper down and removes
her eyeglasses. The years have been good to Tanya.

                     TANYA
           William!

WILLIAM BEAUCHARD, a handsome youth in his early twenties enters the room and embraces Tanya.

                    WILLIAM
          I've missed you, Grandmother.

                    TANYA
          I've missed you, my Harvard man.
                    (beat)
          Did any of the family tag along?

                    WILLIAM
          I gave them the slip.

                    TANYA
                    (laughs)
          I thought the spunk and petered
          out in this family. Then you came
          along. You're the spitting image
          of your great-grandfather.

                    WILLIAM
          Father never speaks of him.

The Butler enters the room.

                    BUTLER
          Madam, dinner is ready.

                    TANYA
          Thank you, George.

Tanya and William walk arm in arm to the door.

TANYA
I want to hear all about your new
job with the Treasury Department.
And afterwards, I'll tell you all about
your great-grandfather, Bogus Beauchard.

FADE OUT.

Made in the USA
Las Vegas, NV
04 February 2022

43139803R00075